Choo Choo

The Runaway Engine

by VIRGINIA LEE BURTON

(Original Title: CHOO CHOO, THE STORY OF A LITTLE ENGINE WHO RAN AWAY)

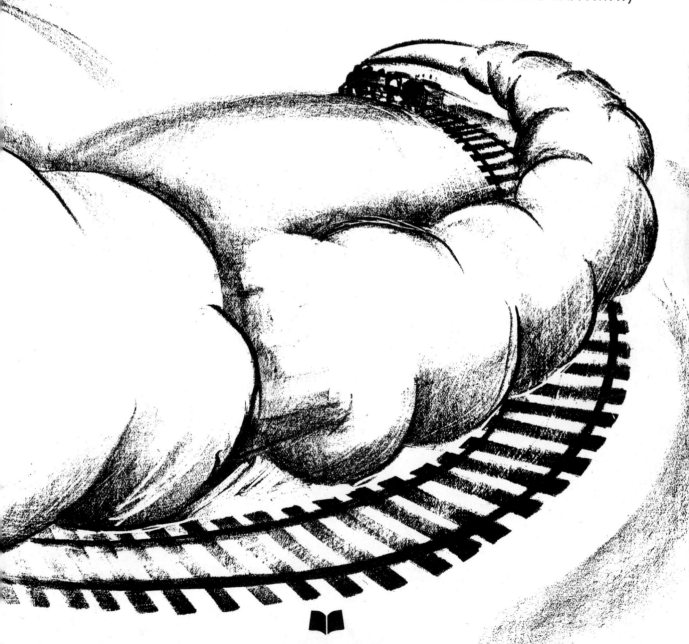

SCHOLASTIC INC.

New York Toronto London Auckland Sydney Tokyo

ISBN 590-04436-2

23 22 21 20 19 18 17 16 15 14 13   8 9/8 0/9

Printed in the U.S.A.   34

TO

MY

SON

ARIS

Once upon a time
there was a little engine.
Her name was CHOO CHOO.
She was a beautiful little engine.
All black and shiny.

CHOO CHOO had a whistle which
went Who WHOOOoo oo oo oo!
when she came to the crossing.

CHOO CHOO had a BELL which
went DING! *DONG!* DING! *DONG!*
when she came to the station.

And a BRAKE which went
s ss ss ss SSSSSWISH!!!
And just made an awful noise.

CHOO CHOO had an engineer.
His name was JIM.
Jim loved the little engine
and took good care of her.
He would shine and polish her till
she looked like new and oil all the
parts so they would run smoothly.

CHOO CHOO had a fireman. His name
was OLEY. Oley fed the little engine
with coal and water. The tender
carried the coal and water.

ARCHIBALD was the conductor who
rode in the coaches. He took the
tickets from the passengers. Archibald
had a big watch. He told the little
engine when it was time to start.

CHOO CHOO pulled all the coaches full
of people, the baggage car full of
mail and baggage and the
tender, from the little
station in the
little town
to the

big station in the big city and back again.

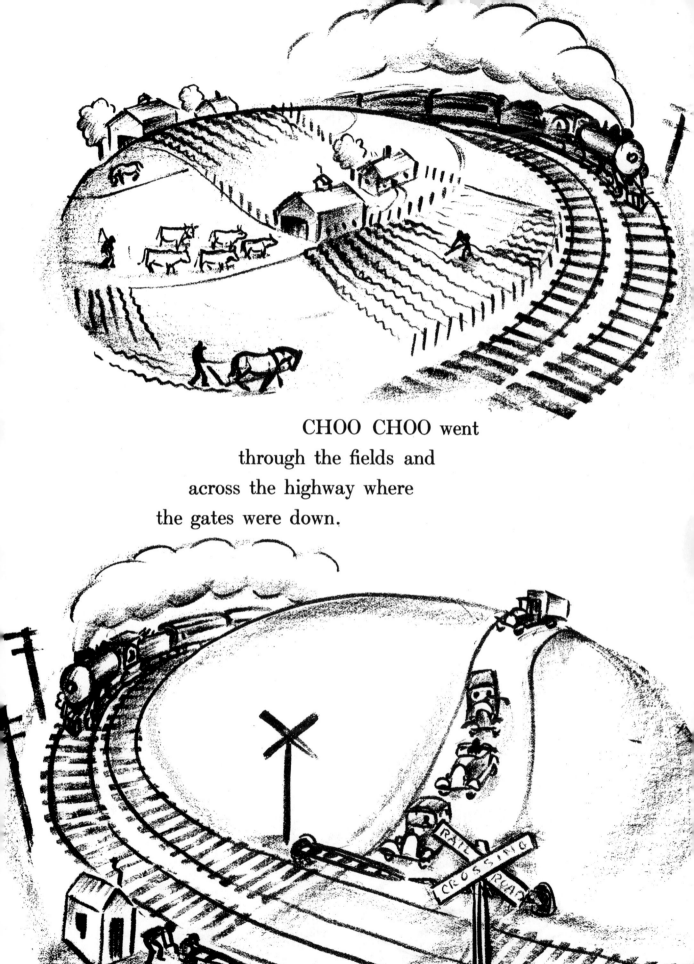

CHOO CHOO went
through the fields and
across the highway where
the gates were down.

CHOO CHOO stopped at the little
stations on the way to pick up
passengers and baggage and
mail to take to the big city.
Ding dong! Ding dong!
And she's off again.
Through the tunnel
and over the hills

Down the hills,
across the drawbridge,

and into the big station
in the big city.

One day CHOO CHOO said
to herself, "I am tired of pulling
all these heavy coaches. I could go
much faster and easier by myself, then all
the people would stop and look at me, just me,
and they would say, 'What a smart little engine!
What a fast little engine! What a beautiful little engine!
Just watch her go by herself!' "

The next day CHOO CHOO was left alone on
the tracks while Jim and Oley and Archibald
were having a cup of coffee in the restaurant.
"Now is my chance!" said CHOO CHOO, and
off she started. CHOO choo choo choo choo
choo! CHOO choo choo choo choo choo!

CHOO choo choo choo! CHOO choo
choo choo! DING dong! DING dong!
Who WHOOOOOOOOOOO! STOP everyone!
LOOK everyone! STOP, LOOK and LISTEN
to ME! CHOO CHOO raced through the fields
and she frightened all the cows and the horses and
the chickens.

CHOO CHOO frightened
all the people and some
clambered up the steeple.
Choo choo CHOO choo!
Choo choo CHOO choo!
Choo choo CHOO choo!
CHOO choo CHOO!

CHOO CHOO whizzed by the crossings.
All the automobiles and trucks had to
put on their brakes so quickly that
they piled one on top of another.
My! they were mad at CHOO CHOO.

Over the hills went the little engine.
Faster and faster. She couldn't stop now
if she wanted to. The drawbridge was up!
CHOO CHOO jumped and just made it.

But
she lost the tender.
Fortunately it fell
on a coal barge
which was passing
under the drawbridge.

CHOO CHOO raced on
into the big yard
in the big city.
Swish! Swish!
went the air brakes
on the express trains.
Poor CHOO CHOO didn't
know which way to turn.
Ah! There was a track out, a
freight track that ran around the city.
CHOO CHOO took it and escaped.

On and on went
CHOO CHOO
out of the city
through the suburbs
and into the country.
It was getting dark! . . .
She had lost her way! . . . .
She did not have much
coal or water left as she
had lost her tender. . . . . . .
Finally she came to where
the tracks divided. .
One track went one
way and the other
track the other way.
She did not know
which track to take
so she took the
track that went
the other way.

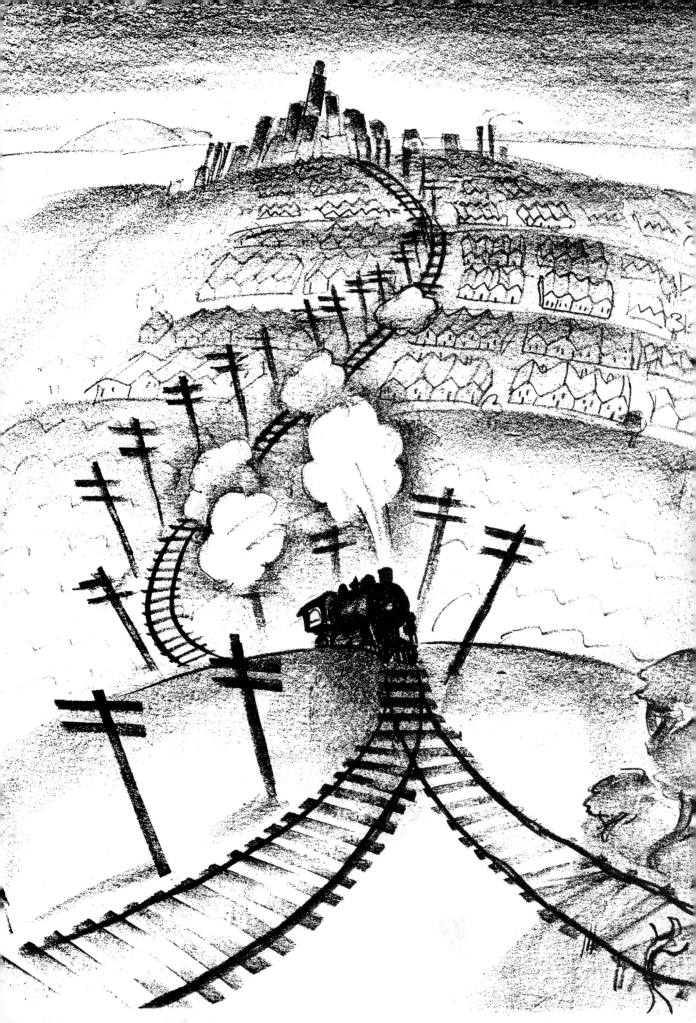

It was an old old track that
hadn't been used for years.
Bushes and weeds had grown
between the ties. The trees
had spread their branches
over it. It was up hill and
almost dark now . . .
and this is how
the poor tired
little engine
went . . . .

CHOOO choo choo choo ch
ch   CHOOoo . . . . choo . . . . . choo
choooo . . . . choo . . . . . . ch . . . . ch
ch . . . . ch . . . . ch . . . . ch
a   a   a   a   a   AH CHOO! And there she sat!

In the meantime
when Jim and Oley
and Archibald heard the
little engine go by they jumped
up and ran after her. Jim called STOP!
STOP! But CHOO CHOO was too far away
to hear even if she wanted to.

Jim and Oley and Archibald
ran and ran till they could
run no more. Just then a
Streamliner train came round
the corner behind them. Jim
took his red handkerchief
and flagged it.

The Streamliner stopped,
Jim called to the Streamliner engineer, "Help
me catch my runaway engine." "What about
my schedule?" said the Streamliner
engineer. "Never mind your
schedule," said Jim. "I
must find CHOO CHOO."
So he climbed in and
Oley and Archibald
followed. Jim took
the controls and
ZOOM!
They were off!

It was easy to
see which way CHOO
CHOO had gone. All the
cows, horses and chickens
pointed with their tails or heads.
The people at the crossing cried out,
"She went that way, that way! Bring her
back!" And the people in the town said, "Hurry!
Hurry! Hurry and catch the little engine, the naughty,
runaway engine before she does any more harm."

While waiting for the drawbridge
  to close, Oley cried out, "Look!
  There's the tender in that coal barge."
Jim said, "Oley and Archibald,
  you stay here and get the tender up.
  I'll go on till I find CHOO CHOO."

Archibald telephoned for the train
derrick. After it came it didn't
take long to get the tender back
on the tracks. They all went on
to the "yard" by the big station
to wait for Jim to come back with
CHOO CHOO.

At last they came
to the place where
the tracks divided.
They didn't know
which way to go
now. While they
were deciding an
old man, who used
to be an engineer
when he was young,
called out to them,
"If you're looking
for a runaway en-
gine she's right up
that track there. And
she won't be far as
it's an old track
which hasn't been
used for well nigh
forty years."

They turned on
the big head light
and went slowly up
the old track. They didn't
go far before they saw the little
engine. CHOO CHOO was so glad to
be found that she blew one "Toot" with
her whistle. There was just enough steam
left for one small "Toot." Jim took a big chain
and ran to the little engine and hooked it on.

The Streamliner backed
down the old track, pulling
CHOO CHOO back to the main
track, back through the big city and
back into the train yard where Oley
and Archibald were waiting.

They attached the tender and ran CHOO CHOO into the
roundhouse and looked her over to see if any damage
had been done. Except for being dusty and
tired she was as good as ever. Jim and
Oley and Archibald were so glad to
have CHOO CHOO back they
danced a jig together.

On the way home CHOO CHOO said
to Jim, "I am not going to run away
any more. It isn't much fun. I am going
to pull all the coaches full of people and the
baggage car from the little town to the big city
and back again."